Joining the Amazing
Club Awesome Sauce

BRAVE
BOOKS

Freedom Island

DOM-A-TRON

Doomsdome

THE OLD ISLANDS

Burrycanter

UTOPIA

WIGGAMORE WO

Rushington

Hive?

SUMA SAVANNA

Furenzy Park

Toke-A-Toke

WonderWell

Capitol

RAKA RAIN FOREST

Mushroom Village

Deserted Desert

Mt. Avalerif

Sky Tree

Snapfast Meadow

CAR-A-LAGO COAST

Starlotte City

Gray Landing

Home of the Brave

Welcome to Freedom Island, Home of the Brave, where good battles evil and truth prevails. Join Ana as she understands the importance of rules and borders when it comes to Club Awesome Sauce. Complete the BRAVE Challenge at the end of the book to learn more!

Watch this video for an introduction to the story and BRAVE Universe!

Saga Three: Tubular
Book 2

Joining the Amazing Club Awesome Sauce

Saga Three: Tubular—Book 2

Joining the Amazing Club Awesome Sauce

Book Illustrations © 2022 by Ali Elzeiny
Map Illustration © 2021 by Ali Elzeiny

Published by BRAVE BOOKS
www.BRAVEbooks.com

ISBN: 978-1-955550-36-9 (paperback)

First edition published in the USA in 2023 by BRAVE BOOKS

Printed in Canada

Joining the Amazing
Club Awesome Sauce

Sara Carter and **BRAVE BOOKS**

Art by **Ali Elzeiny**

Rebel the cheetah was Ana's hero. Rebel was faster than lightning and more fearsome than thunder. Heroes like Rebel probably never had to deal with chores or rules. At Ana's house, there were so many rules.

After dinner, Ana's father reminded her to put away the dishes. Ana sighed, "I bet Rebel doesn't have to follow rules."

Ana's father smiled. "Rebel would surprise you, sweet pea."

"But Dad, her name is *Rebel!* It's like she was born to not follow the rules!"

Ana's father sat down beside her, "Let me tell you a story. Then you can tell me what you think of Rebel."

Years ago, after Rebel's chores were done,
She left her house for some cool summer fun.
She dashed out to play with a skip and a roar,
Through the hills, tall grass, and woods to explore.

This day became special when Rebel heard a sound.
She perked up, gave a sniff, and looked all around.
There was Calvin the Coyote and Kenny the Dog
Building a clubhouse with sticks, twigs, and logs.

Kenny said, "This is way better than swimming at the lake.
Our new treehouse will have rules and a secret handshake.
Rules like: Bring snacks to share, and always raise the flag!
Keep the treasures safe, and don't pick your nose *Gag*."

"I think that you're right," said the coyote kid.

"We should make it official." So they did.

They painted CLUB AWESOME SAUCE on the front door
And wrote out the rules: one, two, three, and four.
Rebel was thrilled when the building was done;
She had never seen a club that looked so fun!

Rebel took a deep breath and strolled right up: Knock, Knock, Knock
"I noticed Club Awesome Sauce and thought we could talk.
Do you think I could join? Your club is so cool."
"ABSOLUTELY!" said Calvin, ignoring the rules.

"Wait," warned Kenny. "To join us you must agree
To follow the rules on the Awesome Sauce Tree."
"Of course," Rebel said, answering with glee.
"I'll follow the rules and bring snacks for us three!"

From then on, Rebel visited every single day.

She brought cookies from home and fresh lemonade.

They built a long shelf for odd treasures and ends.

As time drifted by, they all grew to be friends.

One day a new group asked, "Can we join the crew?"
"You can," answered Rebel, "if you keep the rules, too."
They didn't like the rules, so they grumbled away.
Calvin watched them leave sadly, wishing they'd stay.

Calvin snuck out under the cover of night.

He tip-toed to the club; no one else was in sight.

He tossed a rope through the open back window.

More friends in no time! he told himself, Bingo!

Animals came early, the door was shut tight.
So they climbed up the rope, using all of their might.
But the climb was dangerous. "Try not to fall!"
They yelled as they scaled the clubhouse wall.

Within minutes, the clubhouse was full.

Children yelled down, "Your rules are not cool!"

They tumbled and wrestled. (A rabbit got hurt.)

Then a raccoon threw the rules in the dirt.

The friends saw the stomping and crashing, Whack!
As kids drank up the drinks and ate up all the snacks.
They broke boards, tore things, and crushed Turtle's toe.
A big ol' mean moose smashed treasures Oh no!

"Who let them all in?" Rebel said, wanting to cry.

She and Kenny left the clubhouse with tears in their eyes.

Their clubhouse was wrecked, and it seemed no one cared.
It had been so special, so cool, and it had been theirs.

Calvin had seen enough and left with a frown.

"This is my fault. I've let you both down.

I thought without rules, they'd be fine, they'd be free.

Now I see we need rules. Can you please forgive me?"

Kenny and Rebel nodded. "We forgive you."

They forgave and they hugged because that's what friends do.

When the kids returned, there was no rope to climb.
Calvin told them it would be different this time.
"Hey! These are the rules that you cannot cross,
To join the amazing Club Awesome Sauce."

Some kids agreed that Calvin was right.

So they learned all the rules with joy and delight.

The new friends played inside every single day.

"Club Awesome Sauce is great," they all declared *Yay!*

"You were friends with Rebel, Dad? *The* Rebel?"
Ana burst out, "I can't wait to be just like
her, I'm going to do all my chores before you
can even blink an eye! Do you think we could
rebuild Club Awesome Sauce?"

Kenny laughed, "Yes, sweet pea."

TOKE-A-TOKE TRIBUNE

Issue 2   News of the Toke-A-Toke Area

REBEL FOUND TO BE LINKED TO THE OLD CLUB TREEHOUSE

#1 Place to Eat Goes to Big Bear's Pizza

Based on Tubular rankings of "Top 10 places to eat on Freedom Island," local chef of Toke-A-Toke claims the #1 spot on the list. Big Bear said this in response, "I didn't even know there was a ranking system! I just love making pizza. Discounted pizza for everyone!" Pick up your pizza coupons before they're out!

TOKE-A-TOKE TWISTER

Pretty quick with peculiar pronunciation? Try these tricky tongue twisters!

"Readily ready Rebel reroutes really round rivers."

"Hannah Banana bears a blue bandana. How many bananas upon the blue bandana does Hannah Banana's bandana bear?"

"Kenny and Calvin's crazy club cost Calvin and Kenny a penny."

BRAVE CADETS,

Ana has learned from her father's story, but she still needs help creating her own club and creating her own rules. Complete the three missions below to help her create her club:

- Update your map with the flag sticker included.

- Help Ana in the BRAVE Challenge, and celebrate your victory with an epic reward.

- Can you find the turtle 6 times in the story?

Ana's counting on you! Are you ready to be BRAVE?

Seymour Clues Found Traveling to Starlotte City

Everyone's favorite canine clue finder was spotted off of Car-A-Lago coast, entering Starlotte through the large whirlpool. With a snout capable of sniffing out mysterious cases, who knows what could have led Seymour to Starlotte City?

An aquaintence of the BRAVE Rebel?

Local Toke-A-Toke resident, Kenny, claims to have been in a kid's club with the BRAVE hero Rebel. "It was great! Our club had some guidelines to help make it fun for everyone. But don't let Rebel's name fool you, she followed the club rules very well." Kenny hopes to rebuild the club someday for his daughter Ana.

INTRODUCING...
SARA CARTER

Sara Carter is an investigative reporter, a Fox News Contributor, and has appeared on more than 25 national radio shows. Not only has she won awards for her investigative reports, but she has also received national recognition for her stories that have impacted lives around the world. Sara and her husband, Martin, have six children and live in Texas. She has partnered with BRAVE Books to write *Joining the Amazing Club Awesome Sauce,* and will walk through the tough topic of border control in the BRAVE Challenge.

SARA SUGGESTS:

"I am so excited to be a part of this story on border control! My hope is that your children will understand how border control keeps our country safe."

Border Control: The rules through which the government decides who and what can legally enter the country.

INTRODUCTION

Club Awesome Sauce is in danger! Your mission for this BRAVE Challenge is to protect the club and its important rules. If the BRAVE Cadets can earn 8 points by the end of the games, they've won the challenge and protected the club rules.

Before starting Game #1, choose a prize for winning. For example ...

- Building a clubhouse
- Baking delicious cookies
- Creating a secret family handshake
- Whatever gets your kiddos excited!

GAME #1 - BORDER WATCH

LESSON

When people ignore borders, there is no control of what comes in and out of a country.

OBJECTIVE

Calvin let kids who didn't care about the rules into Club Awesome Sauce. Now the clubhouse is in chaos! BRAVE Cadets, help the animals realize that borders and rules are important to maintaining order.

MATERIALS

Pillows, couch cushions, and one of each item on the Illegal Items List below.

INSTRUCTIONS

Setup

1. Using pillows and couch cushions, have the cadets create a border or short wall across the middle of the room. The height of the wall doesn't matter as long as there is a clear line between both sides of the room.

2. Create 2 teams to be countries. Team 1 (the parents) and Team 2 (the cadets). Team 2 can only have 1-2 players at a time. If necessary, repeat the game to give everyone a turn.

3. The cadets must choose 3 items from the following list. The items that they choose will be illegal to bring into their country. Give these items to the parents.

4. The remaining 3 items will be items that are illegal in the parents' country. Give these items to the cadets.

5. Have the cadets stand against the wall in their country that's the farthest from the border. Have the parents do the same thing in their country.

Illegal Items List

- A toy
- A ball
- A book
- A shoe
- A sock
- A stuffed animal

Gameplay

1. Players will try to carry one illegal item at a time to the other team's country and leave it there without being tagged.

2. Players must cross over the border/wall and not go around it. They may not throw or drop items across the border.

3. If a player is tagged while standing in the other country, he must take the illegal item back into his own country and touch the far wall before starting again. If a player successfully brings over a forbidden item, the other team must try to return the illegal item back to the other team's side.

BRAVE TIP

After the game, make sure to keep out the pillows and couch cushions for the next game!

SCORING

The Brave Cadets earn 2 points for each illegal item they successfully kept out of their country.
Deduct a point every time a player broke a rule.
(For example, throwing an illegal item).
If you played this game twice, record the score from the highest scoring cadets team.

TIME

Rounds last for 3 minutes.

ONE CHILD MODIFICATION

Play this game with one parent and one child. Use only 4 illegal items instead of 6.

TALK ABOUT IT

1. In the game, you had to protect your borders to keep illegal items out of your country. What did you do to protect your country from illegal items? How do countries protect their borders in real life? What are the right ways to protect a border? Wrong ways?

2. What do you think border control means? (Hint: read the definition on page 43). Why would countries not allow certain items or people into their country? Do countries have a right to decide what can and cannot come into their country?

3. What happened when Calvin let the animals into the club? Why would the animals not want to follow any of the club rules? How does that affect a country's border?

4. Why is it dangerous to have no borders between countries? Does that mean we can never let anyone into a country? How can someone come into a country the right way?

SARA SUGGESTS

"Borders protect a country and the people inside it from dangerous items or people that come into the country the wrong way. This is called illegal immigration and can cause problems for the country and the people who are living there legally. There's a process that everyone must follow when going into a country in order to protect the rules and rights that the country has set."

GAME #2 - RULES RULE!

LESSON

Established rules and laws bring order to a community.

OBJECTIVE

Rebel's friends created rules for the club, but the other animals don't seem to want to follow them. BRAVE Cadets, help the animals see why rules are important.

INSTRUCTIONS

1. Move the border from the previous game to one end of the room. Leave enough space for a person to stand between the border and the wall.

2. Have a parent and all of the BRAVE Cadets stand side by side against the wall farthest from the border.

3. Choose one cadet to be Kenny and to stand on the other side of the border, facing everyone.

4. When Kenny gives a command that begins with, "Kenny says," the others must obey. If Kenny doesn't start his instructions with "Kenny says," then the cadets and the parent must NOT follow those instructions.

5. Every time a player correctly follows instructions, take one step closer to the border. Kenny's instructions should not instruct the players to move forward. Only if they follow the directions correctly, do they get to move forward.

6. If a player does not follow the instructions correctly, do not step forward. The person who crosses the border first wins the game!

SCORING

The cadets start with 6 points. Every cadet who follows a command that does not begin with "Kenny says" will lose 1 point.

ONE CHILD MODIFICATION

One parent plays Kenny.

TALK ABOUT IT

1. In the game you had to follow Kenny's instructions to make it across the border. In most countries, there are rules about crossing into another country. Do some people ignore those rules and cross anyway? Is that bad? Why or why not?

2. Why do you think rules are made? How do we know if we should follow those rules? Who's rules should we obey over every other rule?

"Let every person be subject to the governing authorities. For there is no authority except from God, and those that exist have been instituted by God."

Romans 13:1 (ESV)

3. In the story, the animals that Calvin let into the club ignored the rules and ended up destroying their clubhouse. What happened when those animals came back the next day? Why was the club better than before?

SARA SUGGESTS

"Rules maintain order and protection for everyone. When we ignore rules, we can end up hurting others and potentially ourselves, so we must be careful to follow them. For example, when a building is being constructed, there's a rule to always wear a hard hat. The rule is there to protect people from getting hurt if something goes wrong."

4. Give an example of when you ignored a rule. What ended up happening? Was someone there to help you follow the rules? Do we usually want someone to tell us what to do? Why? What might have happened if nobody corrected you?

TALLY UP THE POINTS TO SEE IF YOU WON!

FINAL THOUGHTS FROM SARA

Border control helps protect a country from people who want to enter illegally as well as protects people from dangerous items that could be brought in. For people coming illegally into the country, border control protects them from getting into bad or dangerous situations. Rules are vital for border control to work, and without them, some people would do what they want and could cause problems within that country. Parents, you have the opportunity to explain more in depth to your children about border control and the importance of rules to maintain order.